Disney
Tangled

Rapunzel's
Book of Secrets

This book of secrets

belongs to:

Parragon

Bath New York Singapore Hong Kong Cologne Delhi Melbourne

Rapunzel

Rapunzel is a creative, empowered young woman, who just happens to have been locked in a tower her whole life. She is no damsel in distress - she fills her days with painting, music, reading and lots of other things

Some things you didn't know about this tower-bound teen...

- Rapunzel's parents are the King and Queen, which means she is a princess.

- Rapunzel's golden hair is 70 feet long!

- The healing powers of a magical golden flower passed into Rapunzel's hair when she was born.

- An old woman named Mother Gothel snatched Rapunzel away when she was just a baby and locked her in a soaring tower. Mother Gothel wanted to use Rapunzel's hair to stay young and pretty.

- Rapunzel's best friend is a chameleon named Pascal.

- Every year on her birthday, Rapunzel sees lanterns floating into the sky. She longs to leave the tower and see them in person.

More about Rapunzel!

Finding the artist within...

- Rapunzel loves to paint the walls of the inside of the tower. She paints her dreams and ideas about the outside world.

- She plays guitar and sings too – Rapunzel has a beautiful singing voice.

- Rapunzel loves to knit.

- When she's not busy being creative, Rapunzel does her chores.

- The teenager spends hours brushing and caring for her 70 foot of magical, golden hair.

All About Me

My name is Caira Elliot

This is my signature Caira Elliot

My address is 32 connily green
ballythehane cork city Ireland

My date of birth is 22nd of december 2003

I am 8 years old.

I was born in

~~2003 of findays~~
2003 The bons

8

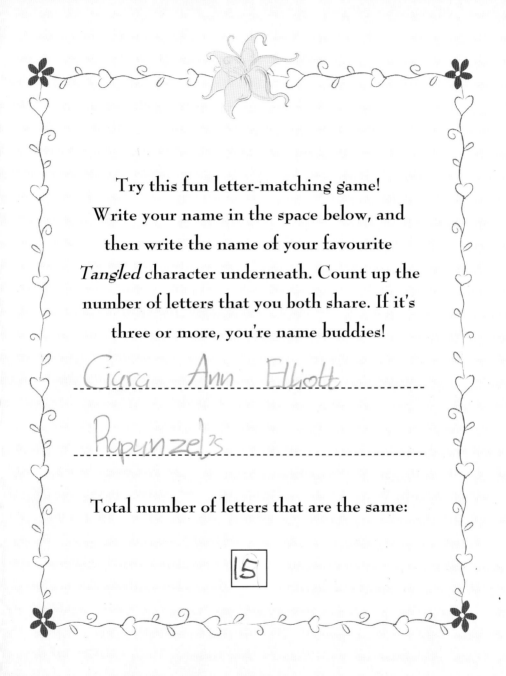

Try this fun letter-matching game!
Write your name in the space below, and
then write the name of your favourite
Tangled character underneath. Count up the
number of letters that you both share. If it's
three or more, you're name buddies!

Ciara   Ann   Elliott

Rapunzel's

Total number of letters that are the same:

15

Flynn Ryder

Flynn Ryder is charming, witty and very good looking. Unfortunately, he's also a thief, and his own biggest fan!

- This ultra-confident charmer relies on his good looks to get out of any sticky situations.

- Unfortunately, Flynn makes a living from stealing. He's looking for his one last, big score that will allow him to live how he's always dreamed.

- Flynn's dream is to buy his own private island and live a life of luxury – but then he meets Rapunzel! He sees her unstoppable spirit and learns there is much more to life.

- Flynn hides in Rapunzel's tower to escape the royal guards' determined horse Maximus.

- His real name is Eugene Fitzherbert.

Identity File

Rapunzel's secret is her magical hair!
What are your identity secrets?

I am:

Left-handed ☐

Right-handed ☑

My shoe size is
~~~~~ 30 or 7½

My hair colour is
~~brown~~ Gold

My eye colour is
Green

My height is
~~~~~ 1m 45cm

A photo of me

Thumbs Up!

Roll your thumb on an ink pad and then press
it down to make a record of your thumbprint here.

A Kiss From Me . . .

Put some lipstick on and then kiss this
page to get a great record of your lip print.

Hint: Leave the book open until the ink and lipstick have dried.

Draw Your Dreams

Rapunzel paints her deepest dreams on the tower walls. Use this page to draw *your* dream - and then make it come true!

DISNEY

Tangled

The Magical Story

Now you can discover the magical story
of the film. Will Rapunzel's dream come
true? Turn the page to find out . . .

Adapted by Lisa Marsoli
Illustrated by Jean-Paul Orpiñas, Studio IBOIX,
and the Disney Storybook Artists

Once upon a time, in a land far away, a drop of sunlight fell to the ground. It grew into a magical golden flower that possessed healing powers. An old woman named Mother Gothel discovered the flower, and hoarded its power to preserve her youth and beauty.

As centuries passed, a glorious kingdom was built close to the cliff where the flower grew. When the beloved queen fell ill, the townspeople searched for the legendary flower, until at last they found it. The flower made the Queen well, and she soon gave birth to a beautiful baby girl. The King and Queen launched a lantern into the sky in celebration.

One night, the vengeful Mother Gothel slipped into the nursery,
where she discovered that the healing power of the flower had transferred
into the baby's golden hair! Mother Gothel cut off a lock – but the hair lost
its power and turned brown. Mother Gothel knew that if she wanted to
stay young, she had to keep the child with her always. She snatched the
princess and vanished to a place where no one could find them. The King
and Queen were heartbroken.

Each year on the Princess's birthday, the King and Queen released
lanterns into the night sky. They hoped their light would guide their
princess home.

Mother Gothel kept Rapunzel locked in a soaring tower and raised her as a daughter. Though the woman pretended to love Rapunzel, she only truly loved Rapunzel's golden hair.

Rapunzel was happy with the companionship of Mother Gothel and her friend Pascal, the chameleon. But she had one dream that she longed to make come true.

On the day before her eighteenth birthday, Rapunzel told Mother Gothel what it was. "I want to see the floating lights!" she said, revealing a painting she had made of them. "They appear every year on my birthday – only on my birthday. And I can't help but feel like they're meant for me!"

Mother Gothel told Rapunzel she was too weak and helpless to handle the outside world. "Don't ever ask to leave this tower again," she said.

Meanwhile, in another part of the forest, a thief named Flynn Rider was on the run with his partners in crime, the Stabbington brothers. Flynn clutched tightly to a satchel that held a stolen royal crown!

Flynn knew the Stabbingtons were too dangerous to be trusted, so he left them and took off with the satchel. But the Captain of the Guard and his horse Maximus were on his heels! The tricky thief knocked the Captain off Maximus and landed in the saddle himself.

Maximus spun in circles until he sunk his teeth into the satchel. As Flynn yanked the satchel free, it went flying into the air.

The satchel snagged on a tree that extended over a cliff. Flynn and Maximus both made their way out onto the tree trunk. But the tree broke, sending the thief and horse toppling into the canyon below.

When they landed, Flynn took off before Maximus could pick up his scent. The thief ducked into a cave. When he emerged from the other side, he saw something amazing: an enormous tower. It would make the perfect hiding place!

He climbed the tower and scrambled into the open window at the top. Finally, he breathed a sigh of relief. He was safe!

CLANG!

Suddenly, everything went black.

Rapunzel had been so startled by the intruder, she snuck up behind him and hit him with a frying pan! Flynn was the first man she had ever seen. He didn't look like the scary ruffians that Mother Gothel had warned her about. Rapunzel thought he was actually pleasant-looking.

After making sure he was unconscious, Rapunzel dragged Flynn to the closet and stuffed him inside. Rapunzel felt exhilarated! Surely this act of bravery would prove to Mother that she could handle herself in the outside world.

Then Rapunzel noticed the mysterious gold object in Flynn's satchel. She placed it on top of her head and gazed into the mirror. She felt different somehow.

Suddenly, Mother Gothel arrived. Rapunzel brought up the floating lights again. She was about to show Mother the stranger in the closet, but Mother cut her off.

"We're done talking about this. You are not leaving this tower! EVER!" roared Mother Gothel.

Ever? Rapunzel was shocked. Realizing she would never get out of the tower unless she took matters into her own hands, Rapunzel asked for another birthday present. She requested special paint that would require Mother to leave on a three-day journey.

Mother Gothel agreed to get the paint and left the tower. Not wasting another second, Rapunzel dragged Flynn out of the closet and offered him a deal. If Flynn took her to see the floating lights and returned her home safely, she would give him the satchel. Flynn had no choice but to agree.

As much as Rapunzel longed to leave the tower, when the moment came, she was terrified. She had never been outside before. But when she glanced back at her painting of the floating lights, Rapunzel overcame her fear and leaped!

With Pascal on her shoulder, she slid down her hair, stopping just inches above the ground. Slowly, Rapunzel touched one foot to the soft grass, then the other.

"I can't believe I did this! I can't believe I did this! I can't believe I did this!" she shouted as she rolled on the ground.

Rapunzel was having the time of her life, but she also felt like a terrible daughter for betraying Mother Gothel. One moment she was running gleefully through a meadow, the next she was sobbing facedown in a field of flowers.

Flynn tried to take advantage of Rapunzel's guilt by making her feel even worse. "Does your mother deserve this?" he asked. "No. Would it break her heart? Of course. I'm letting you out of the deal. Let's turn around and get you home."

Flynn's charms didn't work on Rapunzel.

"I'm seeing those lanterns," she insisted.

Not far from the tower, Mother Gothel came face to face with Maximus.

"A palace horse," she gasped, seeing the kingdom's sun symbol on Maximus' chest. She thought the guards had found Rapunzel. She turned and frantically raced back to the tower.

Mother Gothel searched everywhere, but Rapunzel was gone. Then she saw something shiny beneath the staircase. It was the crown in the satchel, along with Flynn's WANTED poster. Now she knew exactly who had taken Rapunzel – and nothing was going to stop her from finding him!

By this time, Flynn had led Rapunzel to a cosy-looking pub called the Snuggly Duckling. But inside, the place was filled with scary-looking thugs! Flynn was hoping to frighten Rapunzel into returning to the tower.

Then someone held up Flynn's WANTED poster. The pub thugs began fighting for the reward money – with Flynn caught right in the middle of the brawl.

Rapunzel banged her frying pan on a giant pot to get the thugs' attention. She asked them to let Flynn go so that she could make her dream come true. To Rapunzel's surprise, every one of the thugs had a secret dream, too.

Outside, Mother Gothel arrived at the pub. She looked into the window, and was shocked to see that Rapunzel had managed to befriend a room full of ruffians!

Suddenly, Maximus, the royal guards and the captive Stabbington brothers burst into the pub.

"Where's Rider?" demanded the Captain.

One of the thugs revealed a secret passageway to Flynn and Rapunzel. They gratefully disappeared into the dark tunnel.

Moments later, Maximus led the guards straight to the escape route. After they had left, the Stabbington brothers broke free and headed down the passageway themselves. They wanted the crown back!

Mother Gothel had seen everything, and made one of the thugs tell her where the tunnel ended.

Flynn and Rapunzel sprinted through the tunnel and skidded to the edge of an enormous cavern. Rapunzel lassoed her hair around a rock and jumped! She swung over the wide chasm and landed on a stone column. Meanwhile, Flynn fended off Maximus and the guards with Rapunzel's frying pan! Rapunzel tossed her hair to him and held on tight as Flynn swung through the air, right over the Stabbington brothers!

But they weren't safe yet. A dam suddenly burst, filling the entire cavern with water! Maximus, the guards and the Stabbingtons were washed away and Flynn and Rapunzel were trapped in a small cave.

The water quickly began to rise. As Flynn frantically searched for a way out, he cut his hand on the rocks.

"It's pitch black. I can't see anything," he said.

"This is all my fault," Rapunzel said tearfully. "I'm so sorry, Flynn."

"Eugene. My real name's Eugene Fitzherbert," Flynn admitted. "Someone might as well know."

Rapunzel revealed a secret of her own: "I have magic hair that glows when I sing."

Suddenly she realized her hair could light up the cave and show them the way out!

At the tunnel's exit, Mother Gothel waited for Flynn and Rapunzel, but the Stabbington brothers emerged instead. She offered them revenge on Flynn – and something even more valuable than the crown. The Stabbington brothers liked the sound of that!

Meanwhile, Rapunzel, Flynn and Pascal had made it safely to shore and built a campfire for the night. Rapunzel wrapped her hair around Flynn's injured hand and began to sing. Her glowing hair healed Flynn's wound. Flynn was dumbfounded.

He was finally beginning to understand how truly special Rapunzel was.

When Flynn went off to gather firewood, Mother Gothel appeared from the shadows of the woods to take Rapunzel back to the tower.

But Rapunzel refused to go back. "I met someone, and I think he likes me," she said.

Mother Gothel laughed at her. She handed Rapunzel the satchel with the crown and told her that it was all Flynn wanted. Once Rapunzel gave it to him, the thief would vanish. After Mother Gothel set the seeds of doubt, she retreated back into the forest. Rapunzel wanted to trust Flynn but she wasn't sure. She decided to hide the satchel in a nearby tree.

The next morning, Flynn woke up to Maximus trying to drag him away! Rapunzel came to Flynn's rescue and talked the horse into letting the thief go free for one more day.

As Flynn and Maximus shook on their truce, a bell rang in the distance. Rapunzel ran towards it until she came to the crest of a hill. Rapunzel gasped as the entire kingdom came into view. Her dream was just hours away from coming true!

Rapunzel, Flynn, Maximus and Pascal entered the gates of the kingdom. The town was the most exciting thing Rapunzel had ever experienced. A little boy greeted Rapunzel with a kingdom flag that had a golden sun symbol on it. Then a group of little girls braided Rapunzel's locks and pinned them up with flowers. Afterwards, Rapunzel and Flynn joined a crowd as a dance was about to begin.

Rapunzel was transfixed by a the mosaic behind the stage. It was of the King and Queen holding a baby girl with striking green eyes, just like her own.

"Let the dance begin!" called an announcer.

Rapunzel and Flynn joined hands and began to whirl around the square.

After they danced, the couple visited shops and enjoyed the sights. All the while, they were getting to know each other better. It was a wonderful day!

As evening approached, Flynn led Rapunzel to a boat and rowed them to a spot with a perfect view of the kingdom.

As lanterns filled the sky, Rapunzel's heart soared. She gave Flynn the satchel, which she had kept hidden all day. She was no longer afraid he would leave her once he had the crown.

Beneath the glow of the lanterns, Rapunzel and Flynn held hands and gazed into each other's eyes.

Their romantic moment ended abruptly when Flynn spotted the Stabbington brothers watching them from the shore. Quickly, he rowed the boat to land.

"I'll be right back," he told Rapunzel as he grabbed the satchel and strode off.

Flynn gave the brothers the crown, but they wanted Rapunzel and her magic hair instead! He turned to go to Rapunzel, but the brothers knocked him unconscious, tied him to the helm of a boat and set him sailing into the harbour.

Then they came for Rapunzel. The brothers told her that Flynn had traded her for the crown. Rapunzel saw Flynn sailing away. She thought he had betrayed her!

Rapunzel ran off into the forest with the brothers in pursuit. Moments later, she heard Mother Gothel's voice. She ran back and found Mother standing over the unconscious Stabbingtons.

"You were right, Mother," said Rapunzel tearfully, hugging her tight.

Flynn's boat continued to sail until it crashed into a dock. Two guards found him holding the stolen crown and immediately dragged him off to prison.

Maximus was watching nearby. He had witnessed everything and knew he had to do something to save both Flynn and Rapunzel.

As Flynn was led down the prison corridors by the guards, he spotted the Stabbington brothers in a nearby cell. They admitted that Mother Gothel had told them about Rapunzel's hair and eventually double-crossed them.

Suddenly, the pub thugs from the Snuggly Duckling arrived and broke Flynn out of jail! They launched him over the prison walls and onto Maximus' back. Maximus had planned the entire escape! Flynn thanked him and, together, the heroes galloped off to rescue Rapunzel!

Back at the tower, Rapunzel sat in her bedroom, heartbroken. She held up the kingdom flag with the sun symbol and gazed at her wall of art. Then she noticed something amazing. She had been painting the sun symbol her whole life. She suddenly came to the realization that she was the lost princess!

Mother Gothel tried to justify her actions, but Rapunzel no longer believed her lies. Before Rapunzel could reach the window, Mother Gothel overpowered her.

Flynn finally arrived at the tower. "Rapunzel! Rapunzel, let down your hair!" he called.

Rapunzel's golden locks fell to the ground and Flynn began to climb. When he reached the top, he found Rapunzel chained in the middle of the room. He went to help her, but Mother Gothel wounded him with a dagger.

Rapunzel was desperate to save Flynn. She begged Mother Gothel to allow her to heal him. In return, Rapunzel promised Mother Gothel she would stay with her forever.

Mother Gothel agreed to the deal and unchained Rapunzel. She knew Rapunzel never broke a promise, but she chained Flynn to the wall to ensure he wouldn't follow them.

Rapunzel rushed to Flynn's side and placed her hair over his wound.

"No, Rapunzel, don't do this," begged Flynn.

"I'll be fine," said Rapunzel, looking into Flynn's eyes. "If you're okay, I'll be fine."

Flynn caressed her cheek. Then he suddenly reached for a shard of broken glass and cut off her hair! It instantly turned brown and lost its magic healing power.

"What have you done?!" Mother Gothel cried. Within moments she aged hundreds of years and turned to dust.

Rapunzel cradled Flynn in her arms and began to weep. A single golden tear fell upon Flynn's cheek. To Rapunzel's astonishment, the tear – and then Flynn's entire body – began to glow.

Flynn was healed. "Rapunzel!" he exclaimed.

The two embraced and shared their first kiss.

Flynn, Pascal and Maximus brought Rapunzel straight to the castle. Her parents rushed to hug her. They were filled with joy. Their daughter had finally been returned to them! Rapunzel felt her parents' love surround her as they all hugged each other tightly, a family once more.

Soon, all of the townspeople gathered for a welcome home party. The King and Queen were there, along with Flynn, Pascal, Maximus and the pub thugs. The people of the kingdom released floating lanterns into the sky. Their light had guided their princess home at last.

Be Creative!

No matter what happens,
I'm never bored.
There's always a treasure,
To be explored . . .

Rapunzel learns a lot about herself and the world through her imagination, and you can too. On the next few pages you'll find some creative secrets to get you started!

Painting

- Close your eyes and let your imagination run free, then paint what you see!

- Use bright, bold colours that will stand out and look magical.

- Paint your dreams and then make them come true!

Making Music

- You can sing everywhere you go! Use your imagination and sing whatever is in your heart.

- The more you smile while you sing, the prettier your voice will sound.

- Try singing your own words, or practise your favourite song until you know it off by heart.

- Learning an instrument, like the guitar, is another way to make magical music. Rapunzel plays the guitar and sings along while she strums.

Writing Poetry

Picture a scene in your head, and then write down what you see. Try to make the last words of each line rhyme.

Perhaps I am not as I seem,
I have a true and special dream...

My Biggest Secrets

These two pages are for your *really* private secrets. Once you have filled them in, put these pages together and place a tiny piece of invisible tape along the top. If anyone finds your book, they won't notice your hidden pages – they'll be as hidden as Mother Gothel's tower!

My biggest secret is . . . .
. . . .
. . . .

My secret dream is . . . .
. . . .
. . . .

One person I secretly like is . . . .
. . . .

One thing I secretly like is . . . .
. . . .
. . . .

Something I only do in secret is . . . .

. . . .

. . . .

Something I would secretly like to do is . . . .

. . . .

. . . .

One secret I have shared is . . . .

. . . .

. . . .

My Favourite Things

Scribble down your favourite things
quickly to reveal your true thoughts.

Colour
purple
Blue

Number
8
6

Animal
dog

Insect
butterfly

Hobbies
hairdresser
teacher
dancing
singing

Best Friends
Emma
Emma
Holly
Abbie
Rebecca
Gemma
Jessica
Hayley
Courtney and R...
Shannon

Song

~~What makes you bubiful~~
Despacito

Book

A story a day
Isle of the Lost

Drink

. . . Santa . . Lemon . .

Smell

. . . roses . . . .

Music group

. . . One . . D . . . . .

Food

. . . Pizza . . . .

Game

~~Jumping Show~~
Colour Switch

Flower

. . . roses . . . .

Secret Dreams

Rapunzel has many wishes and dreams that she hopes
will come true in the outside world, when she's older.
Write *your* most secret wishes on these pages.

My Dreams Come True...

When I grow up I hope to be *a dancer/singer*

I dream of living in *Marbella (spain)*

My one true love will be *Niall Horan*

If I have children I will call them:

Boy *Dylan*

Girl *Sophiea*

When I Am Older . . .

I will wear . . . .

. . . .

. . . .

. . . .

This is what I
would like to
look like...

My Holiday

Fill in this space with notes about your last holiday. Stick in tickets and photos. Write about the *places* you visited and the *people* you met.

Inside the Tower

This is the place Rapunzel has called home her whole life. She knows *almost* all of its secrets!

- The tower is hidden in a deep, secret valley.

- The only way into the valley is through a secret tunnel.

- Flynn Ryder finds the tower and thinks it's the perfect hiding place!

- The tower is home to Rapunzel, Mother Gothel, and Rapunzel's best friend – a chameleon called Pascal!

- Mother Gothel uses Rapunzel's long hair to enter the tower. She calls "Rapunzel! Let down your hair!" and then the teen pulls her up to the high window.

- Rapunzel could leave the tower at any time, using her long hair, but she never leaves because Mother Gothel tells her the outside world is a scary place.

- Rapunzel doesn't know there is a secret door to get in and out of the tower!

All About Pascal

Learn some secrets about Rapunzel's best friend.

- Pascal is a chameleon and Rapunzel's closest companion.

- The colour of Pascal's skin changes to match his surroundings, so he's very good at hiding!

- Although he's very small, Pascal plays a big part in Rapunzel's life. She shares her deepest dreams and thoughts with Pascal and he knows her better than anyone else.

- Rapunzel takes Pascal along when she escapes from the tower. He is a good and true companion.

- Pascal soon becomes good friends with Maximus, the palace horse that tries to capture Flynn Ryder.

- Pascal loves to see Rapunzel happy. When she goes on a boat ride with Flynn, Pascal looks on with a big smile.

All About Maximus

Find out more about the royal horse with a mission!

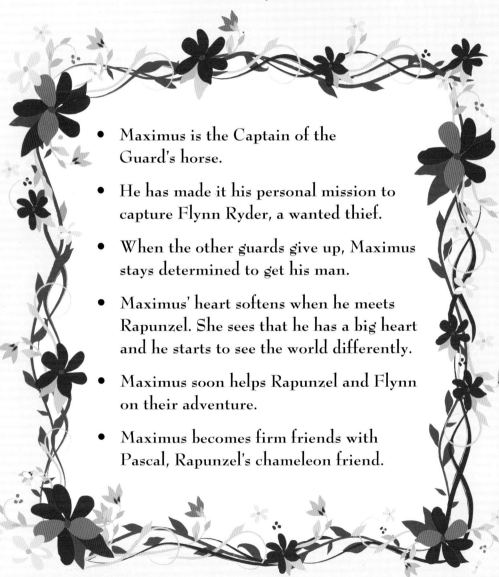

- Maximus is the Captain of the Guard's horse.

- He has made it his personal mission to capture Flynn Ryder, a wanted thief.

- When the other guards give up, Maximus stays determined to get his man.

- Maximus' heart softens when he meets Rapunzel. She sees that he has a big heart and he starts to see the world differently.

- Maximus soon helps Rapunzel and Flynn on their adventure.

- Maximus becomes firm friends with Pascal, Rapunzel's chameleon friend.

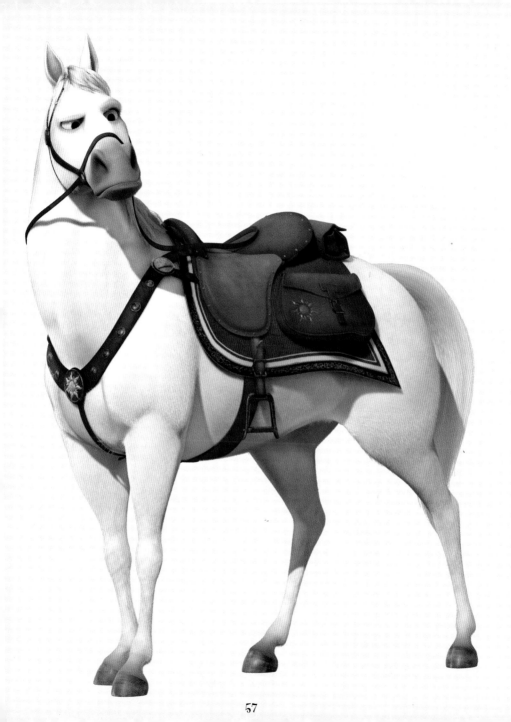

My Favourite Food

A healthy diet will help your hair
look as shiny as Rapunzel's.

What I like to eat

Breakfast .Pancake. . . . .

. . . .

Lunch Crisp Sandwich. . . . .

. . . .

Evening meal .Pizza. . . . .

. . . .

Eat lots of fruit and vegetables every day to help keep yourself healthy. Also drink plenty of water.

Snacks Cakes\ apple Pie

Drinks Fanta Lemon

Yummy or Yuck?

My favourite food Pizza and Strawberry ice cream

My least favourite food brussel sprouts

Ask an adult
to help you!

Rapunzel's Sunset Soup

Ingredients:

1 Onion
2 Leeks
1 Clove of garlic
450g Carrots
1tbsp Olive oil
2 tbsp Butter
3 ½ Cups vegetable stock
Grated rind and juice of 2 oranges
Salt and pepper
1tbsp Chopped fresh parsley

Method:

1. Peel the onion and leeks and finely chop them. Peel and crush the garlic. Peel the carrots and chop into cubes.
2. Heat the oil and butter in the pan over a medium heat. Add the onions and garlic and fry gently for 2-3 minutes.
3. Add the remaining vegetables and continue to cook for a further 2 minutes.
4. Pour in the stock. Cover with a lid and simmer over a low heat for 15-20 minutes.
5. Remove the pan from the heat. Blend with a hand blender until smooth.
6. Add the orange juice and salt and pepper. Serve in warm bowls garnished with orange rind and chopped parsley.

Dear Diary...

Ssshhh . . . on these pages you can read Rapunzel's secret diary from her days locked inside the tower.

Monday

Today I woke just as the sun was rising above the valley. The view was incredible from the high windows and the sight made me think about my dream - to one day go and see the floating lights. I'm scared because Mother Gothel says it's dangerous out there, but one day I will make my dream come true.

Rapunzel

Tuesday

The weather wasn't so lovely today. It rained all morning, so I talked to Pascal about my dream once I had done my chores. He loves to sit and listen and I love to confide in him. Mother Gothel then asked me to sing for her. Singing always makes me feel happy!
Rapunzel.

Wednesday

Today was my birthday, and tonight I saw magical lights in the sky again! They have appeared every year on the evening of my birthday for as long as I can remember, and I'm longing to know what they are. To see them close up would be so exciting! One day I'm going to ask Mother Gothel if I can leave the tower and find those lights.
Rapunzel

Thursday

I'm just about to go to bed, feeling very tired after a day spent painting. I covered the walls with images of those lights I saw on my birthday. I also painted flowers and beautiful scenery. My imagination was working hard today! The time flew by and evening seemed to come very quickly. I can't stop smiling as I look at my paintings - they remind me of my dreams.
Rapunzel

Friday

Today was a music day. I played my guitar all morning and wrote some song words, then sang as I did my chores this afternoon. I love the sound my guitar makes - and so does Pascal it would seem! He was jigging around to the music. I need to practise more so I can be even better at the guitar.
Rapunzel

Saturday

Most of today was taken up with hair care! I've let it
get in a bit of a state this week, so I spent a few hours
brushing all the knots out. Now it feels silky and smooth.
I asked Mother Gothel about the outside world today, but
she tells me I shouldn't keep asking. She says it's scary
and dangerous outside. She says it wouldn't be safe for
me to leave the tower, and I suppose she's right... Thank
goodness I have plenty of things to do to fill my days!
Rapunzel

Sunday

I filled up the hours today with chores, cooking, a bit of
ballet, papier-mache, chess, pottery, drawing, sewing...
the list goes on! I thought all day about being able to see
those floating lights up close. I shouldn't complain - I
have Mother Gothel's love, what more should I want? But
I can't help dreaming of seeing those floating lights up
close, just once...   Rapunzel

Special Friends

Rapunzel's best friend is Pascal, the chameleon. Who are you best friends? Record your special friendships here.

My Best Buddies

Name Emma Daly

Address 12 St. Anns park tunners cross

087 0575167

Telephone number ~~087 9171128~~ ~~021 4320319~~

E-mail Mickey Daly 2010 @ gmail. com

Birthday 10/10/2003

Name Holly Nagle

Address

Telephone number

E-mail

Birthday 10/11/2003

Stick photos of your friends on this page
and write down what they are really good at!

abbe

This is ..Abby..........

Really good at..Singing....

..dancing...laughing..

This is ....

Really good at...........

....

abbie

This is ....

Really good at...........

....

abbie

This is ....

Really good at...........

....

Crazy About Birthdays

Rapunzel's birthday is very important to her, because every year she sees the floating lights that eventually lead her home. Your birthday is important too! The date you were born can reveal all sorts of secrets about the real you . . .

Month	Lucky Stone	Lucky Colour
January	garnet	turquoise
February	amethyst	silver
March	aquamarine	red
April	diamond	brown
May	emerald	orange
June	pearl	yellow
July	ruby	gold
August	sardonyx	purple
September	sapphire	pink
October	opal	blue
November	topaz	black
December	turquoise	green

You're a Star!

Aquarius
January 20th-
February 18th
You are good at coming
up with ideas.

Pisces
February 19th-
March 20th
You are sensitive
and artistic.

Aries
March 21st-
April 20th
You are a leader
and full of energy.

Taurus
April 21st-
May 21st
You are strong
and reliable.

Gemini
May 22nd-
June 21st
You are good at
solving problems.

Cancer
June 22nd-
July 22nd
You are caring
and dependable.

Leo
July 23rd-
August 22nd
You are generous
and confident.

Virgo
August 23rd-
September 22nd
You are logical
and tidy.

Libra
September 23rd-
October 22nd
You are charming
and peace-loving.

Scorpio
October 23rd-
November 21st
You are very
determined.

Sagittarius
November 22nd-
December 21st
You are independent
and smart.

Capricorn
December 22nd-
January 19th
You are hard-
working and
organized.

69

Important Birthdays

Make a note of special
birthdays here.

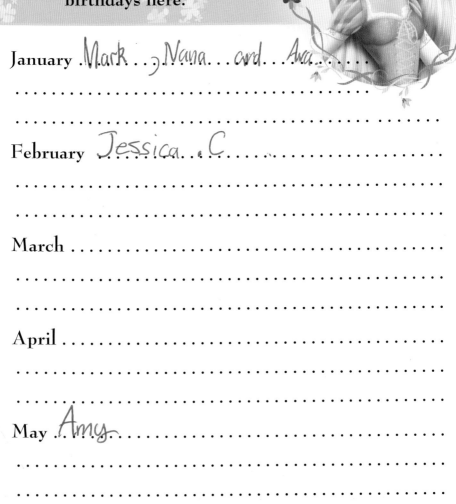

January .Mark ..,.Nana ...and ...Ava...... .
. . . .
. . . .

February .Jessica ..C............... .
. . . .
. . . .

March . . . .
. . . .
. . . .

April . . . .
. . . .
. . . .

May ..Amy.. . . . .
. . . .
. . . .

June . . . .

. . . .

. . . .

July . *Dad* . . . .

. . . .

. . . .

August . *Mam , Granda , Mllll, Mel , ABBIE* . .
Abbie . . . .

. . . .

September . . . .

. . . .

. . . .

October . *❋ , Emma ♡ ❋* . . . .

. . . .

. . . .

November . *Holly , Abby , Michelle* . . . .

. . . .

. . . .

December . *Me , ~~Elo~~ Chloe* . . . .

. . . .

. . . .

Throw a *Tangled* Party!

Throwing a party with a *Tangled* theme will make it even more enjoyable! Ask your friends to dress up as their favourite character.

Decorations

Try to make your house look like the kingdom as it celebrates the birthday of the lost princess. Use beautiful balloons and streamers. Put a colourful paper tablecloth on the table and see if you can find paper napkins to match.

Fancy Food

Ask your parents to make a banquet fit for true *Tangled* fans! Anything delicious and prettily decorated will look great!

Pass the Parcel

Before the party make a 'pass the parcel' with mini *Tangled* presents, like hair clips or paints, between each layer of tissue paper.

Rapunzel's Party Game

Before the party, make a pile of lanterns out of cardboard and hide them around the house. When your guests arrive, ask them to go on a lantern hunt! The guest who finds the most can be given a special prize.

Party Bags

When the party is over, give each of your guests a party bag to take home – full of sweets, treats and *Tangled* gifts!

It's Party Time!

Party Invitation

You'll need some plain paper or thin card, pens, ruler, scissors, a coffee mug and a butterfly paper fastener.

1 Draw twice round the mug on to some card to make two circles. Cut them out. Fold one circle in half and then half again.

2 Open it up. The fold lines will mark the quarters and middle of the circle. Cut a v-shape out of one quarter – not quite reaching the centre of the circle.

cut out

3 Put the two circles together (put the one with the cut out v-shape on the top). Push the paper fastener through the middle and open it out at the back.

4 Turn the top circle round and write your invitation details in each quarter. Decorate the top with a picture of Rapunzel.

Guest List & Party Music

People to invite: . . . .
. . . .
. . . .
. . . .
. . . .

Party Music
You need music for a good party!
Make a note of your top 5 party songs.

Song 1 . . . .

Song 2 . . . .

Song 3 . . . .

Song 4 . . . .

Song 5 . . . .

Rapunzel's Hair Care Secrets

With 70 foot of the stuff, Rapunzel knows a thing or two about hair. Here are her top tips on keeping it silky and beautiful!

How to Wash Your Hair

1. Wet hair with warm (not boiling!) water.
2. Squeeze a small amount of shampoo into your hand and massage into your scalp. Massage with your fingertips (not your nails).
3. Start at your scalp and move out toward the ends of your hair.
4. Rinse out the shampoo well.
5. If you need conditioner, squeeze some into your hand (more if your hair is very long). Apply to the ends of your hair and leave in a minute or two.
6. Rinse well.

- The best way to keep your hair looking shiny is to gently brush it every day.

- Washing your hair gets rid of dirt, oils and products. It's best to wash your hair every other day – doing it more often can take away some of your hair's natural goodness.

- If your hair needs it, use a conditioner after washing. This will smooth your hair and make it look shiny.

- Have your hair cut every six weeks to keep it in excellent condition – don't try doing it yourself!

- Protect your hair with a hat if you're going out into the bright sunshine.

- Don't wear a ponytail every day. Once a week, give your hair a break and let it hang free!

Secret Dreams

Rapunzel isn't the only one who has dreams.
Everyone dreams when they are asleep. Do you remember
any of yours? If you write them down as soon as you wake
up, it will help you remember them for longer.

Date of Dream: . . . .

Who was in it: . . . .

What it was about: . . . .

. . . .

Was it a nice dream?   Yes ☐   No ☐

Date of Dream: . . . .

Who was in it: . . . .

What it was about: . . . .

. . . .

Was it a nice dream?   Yes ☐   No ☐

Date of Dream: . . . .

Who was in it: . . . .

What it was about: . . . .

. . . .

Was it a nice dream?   Yes ☐   No ☐

My Secret Memories

Use this page to record all the special things that happen to you during the year. Glue in photographs and mementos of any special occasion.

How Embarrassing!

Embarrassing moments happen to everybody,
even talented Rapunzel. Write your moments on these
pages, and they might not seem not so bad after all!

**The most embarrassing thing that ever happened to me
was** . . . .

. . . .

. . . .

. . . .

. . . .

The most embarrassing thing I ever wore was . . . .

. . . .

. . . .

. . . .

The most embarrassing thing anyone ever said to me was

. . . .

. . . .

. . . .

The things that most embarrass me about my family are

. . . .

. . . .

. . . .

. . . .

One thing I wish I had never done is . . . .

. . . .

. . . .

. . . .

. . . .

My worst habit is. . . . .

. . . .

. . . .

. . . .

. . . .

. . . .

Presents

When you are given lots of presents on special occasions, it's easy to forget who gave you what! So why don't you make a list here, so you don't get in a muddle with your thank-you letters?

Present:

From:

. . . .

. . . .

. . . .

. . . .

. . . .

. . . .

. . . .

. . . .

. . . .

. . . .

. . . .

. . . .

. . . .

. . . .

. . . .

. . . .

. . . .

Which *Tangled* Character Are You?

Answer the questions to see which *Tangled* character is most like you. Make a note of your answers, then check the results on the opposite page.

1. **How would you rather spend your day?**

   a) Singing and playing guitar.
   b) Chasing down a wanted thief!
   c) Listening to your best friend.
   d) Counting your stash of jewels and money.

2. **Which of these is closest to your own dream?**

   a) To explore the world outside of your window.
   b) To achieve an important mission.
   c) To see your best friend's dream come true.
   d) To live a life of luxury on your own private island.

3. **What is your favourite hobbie?**

   a) Anything creative!
   b) Catching wanted thieves.
   c) Hiding, and helping your best friend.
   d) Causing trouble.

4. Which of these sentences best describes you?

   a) Getting more independent every day.
   b) Determined and strong.
   c) A true and loyal friend.
   d) Witty and charming.

Results

Mostly A – You are Rapunzel. You are creative and curious.

Mostly B – You are Maximus. Determined and big hearted.

Mostly C – You are Pascal. You are a perfect friend.

Mostly D – You are Flynn Ryder. Troublesome yet charming.

Create a Secret Tangled Code!

Choose a secret symbol for each letter in the alphabet –
perhaps a floating lantern or a picture of Pascal!

Real letters	A	B	C	D	E	F
My code	B	D	Q	A	C	E.

Real letters	G	H	I	J	K	L
My code `	G	I	J	K	H	L

Real letters	M	N	O	P	Q	R
My code	M	Q	P	R	N	Q

Real letters	S	T	U	V	W	X
My code	T	V	X	S	U	W

Real letters	Y	Z
My code	Z	Y

Write a secret message on this page,
using your special Tangled code!

**Remember: Don't tell anyone except your
closest friends how to crack your code.**

Tangled Quiz!

How many of Rapunzel's secrets do you know?
Take this *Tangled* quiz and find out! Turn the book upside
down to see how many you got right.

1. Who locked Rapunzel in the hidden tower?
   Mother Gothel

2. What type of animal is Pascal?
   A chameleon

3. What is Flynn Ryder's real first name?
   Eugene

4. How long is Rapunzel's magical hair?
   70 foot

5. What is hidden in Flynn's satchel?
   A crown

6. What are the lights in the sky that
   Rapunzel sees on her birthday?
   floating Lanterns

90

7. How old is Rapunzel when she finally sees the floating lights at the Kingdom?

Eighteen

8. Who are Rapunzel's real parents?

The King, and Queen Queen

Secret Notes

Dream like this...
Like the song &
dance

.hoewdown

realy like the song and
love the dance,
lego heuse.
The song is brilliaut

Use these pages for your own secret notes, and to
practise the creative tips Rapunzel has taught you!

Ciara

metting tomorow

at 3oclock

she is

till 9 Pm night

Miss Jorgan

My favourite page in this book was:

....

My favourite secret about Rapunzel is:

....

The page I found hardest to complete was:

....

Something I discovered about myself was:

....